Fergus's Big Splash

To my granddchildren:
Natalie, Zara, Chloe, Holly, Olivia and Jamie

First published in 1996 in Great Britain by
Piccadilly Press Ltd, London
www.piccadillypress.co.uk

Text and illustrations copyright © Tony Maddox 1996

This 2010 edition published by Sandy Creek by arrangement with Piccadilly Press

Sandy Creek
122 Fifth Avenue
New York, NY 10011

ISBN: 978 1 4351 2330 4

1 3 5 7 9 10 8 6 4 2

Printed and bound in China

Fergus's Big Splash

Tony Maddox

Sandy Creek

Fergus was looking for Farmer Bob.
He wasn't in the hayfield.

He wasn't in the big barn.

Fergus asked the animals.
"Moo!" said the cow.
"Oink, Oink!" suggested the pigs.
"Cluck, Cluck, Cluck!" added the hen.
"Quack, Quack!" agreed the ducks.

"Humph!" thought Fergus.
"He must have gone fishing!"
So he went to look.
And the cow, the three pigs,
the two ducks and the hen
followed him...

...through the tall grass of the meadow...

…over the fence and into the dark woods…

…until they came to the big pond.
Fergus climbed into an old boat
docked by the bank, to get
a better view.
The cow climbed in after him, followed
by the three pigs, the two ducks and
the hen.

The boat drifted to the middle of the pond.
The animals Mooed and Oinked and
Quacked and Clucked and the boat rocked.
Everyone was having a great time...
...except Fergus!

"I wish they would keep still!"
he worried.

But they didn't...
and the boat rocked more...and more
and more...until SPLASH!

It tipped over completely, tumbling everyone into the water.

Farmer Bob awoke with a start.
He'd fallen asleep in the shade
of a big tree. "What's that?" he said.
He turned to see...

the cow paddling in the water,
the pigs rolling in the mud,
the ducks playing in the reeds,
the hen pecking in the grass...
and a very wet Fergus!

"Fergus," said Farmer Bob.
"What have you been up to?"
The other animals gathered around.
It looked like Fergus was in trouble.

"Well," thought Fergus.
"At least I found Farmer Bob!"
And he shook himself dry and trotted
back to the farm.

That was the second soaking
the animals had that day!